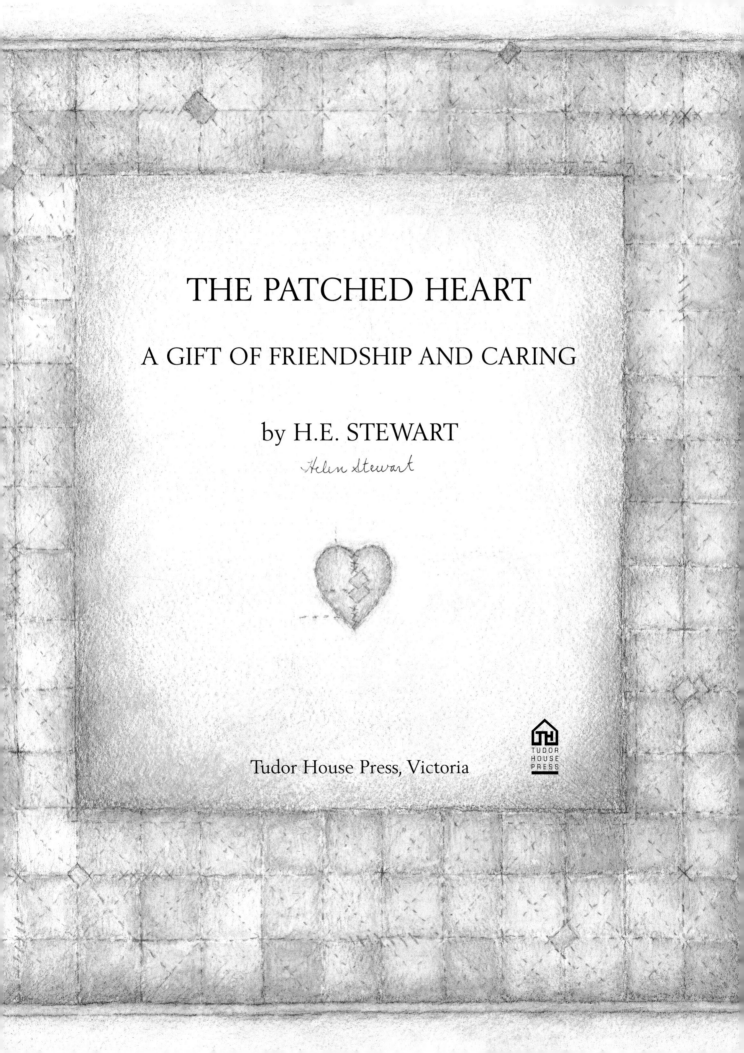

THE PATCHED HEART

A GIFT OF FRIENDSHIP AND CARING

by H.E. STEWART

Helen Stewart

Tudor House Press, Victoria

TUDOR HOUSE PRESS

Library and Archives Canada Cataloguing in Publication

Stewart, H.E. (Helen Elizabeth), 1943-
   The patched heart : a gift of friendship and caring / H.E. Stewart.

ISBN 978-0-9693852-5-7

   I. Title.
PS8587.T4855P38 2007   jC813'.54   C2006-904911-4

PRINTED IN CANADA

Tudor House Press is committted to reducing the consumption of ancient forests.
This book is one step towards that goal. It is printed on acid-free paper that is
100% ancient forest free, and has been processed chlorine free.

Over many years, I have had several dogs who were more than good friends and companions.

They were herders and helpers, guardians and protectors. When not working, they were full of fun, and then they rested content.

These dogs were teachers, too, of caring, compassion and trust.

I thank each one.

There once was a time....

Two puppies ran together along the beach,
scattering sunlight and seawater – and feeling
fine.

Suddenly a terrible pain, like a giant wave, crashed down on Big Puppy. He crumpled to the ground with his heart hurting, and there he lay, stone-still, hardly breathing.

His little friend was so afraid. For Mossy, the sky had fallen and now darkness crept close. She whimpered and whined and cried out her distress.

Farther along the beach, the Newfie dogs were keeping watch. This was their job. Whenever the alarm sounded, they hurried to the rescue. Now they found Big Puppy.

Using the teamwork needed in emergencies, they lifted him onto a stretcher and carefully carried him to the nearby clinic.

Doctor Elephant promptly examined him.
(With her l–o–n–g trunk and her B-I-G ears,
she was an especially good listener.)

She declared Big Puppy's heart badly
damaged, and quickly called for an ambulance.

Big Puppy was rushed away to the hospital.
It was frightening! The siren hurt his ears, and
besides that, little Mossy had been left behind
by mistake!

No one realized how important she was. No
one knew how very loyal she was. Her heart
was set on staying with her friend. She climbed
up high to see which way to follow. Then off
she bounded like a rippling of wind, in the
same direction as the ambulance.

Big Puppy was confused. To him, everything seemed strange. After all, he had never been away from home before. He was feeling bad, and the smells and sounds at the hospital made him feel even worse.

Nurses came to take his temperature and his
blood pressure. Doctors came to listen to his heart.
There were tests and more tests.

Then he was taken to the operating room. His nurse explained that she would give him medicine so he would fall fast asleep. Then the doctors could patch his heart.

Big Puppy did not remember anything more.

He awoke all alone in the darkness. He was frightened,
like a fish caught in a net, with lines attached to machines
all busily beeping and squeaking. He could not understand
what was happening. He lay very still, for fear of tangling
the lines.

After a time, somewhere between sleeping and waking,
he heard a faint but familiar scratching noise at his door.

In crept Mossy – like a dream shadow, only real. And
now Big Puppy did not feel afraid anymore.

The next morning, the head nurse was very stern when she discovered Mossy. "No visitors allowed except during proper visiting hours!" she barked. (She was by nature very orderly.)

Mossy, however, paid no attention. (She was by nature very devoted.)

She crept back again —

and again —

and again.

But being just a young puppy, she did not understand about hiding.

At last the nurse gave in and decided to let her stay. And that is when Big Puppy began to feel better.

Big Puppy was a long time in the hospital. In the beginning he was always sleepy and mostly napping. Other times he lay quiet and uncomplaining. The nurses called him by a pet name now. They called him Patch.

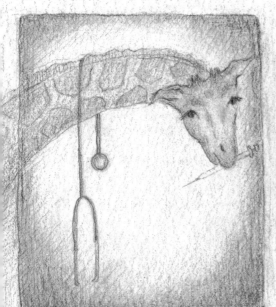

Mossy sometimes kept watch – and sometimes went off to visit more lively and wide-awake patients.

Whenever Patch was awake, a nurse appeared with a pill (which was hard to swallow) or a shot (which did not feel good). Mossy

offered encouragement in these trying times, cheering Patch when he did not spit out his pills. She tried to make up for his troubles – and for the hospital food – by bringing in treats.

As Patch recovered, his friends were
allowed short visits, but only during proper
visiting hours, and never when he was
napping or taking his medicine.

Other patients also ventured in to visit.
They, of course, had heard all about Patch
from Mossy.

A hospital is a busy place, making it difficult to rest. Patch grew weary of the constant coming and going, the lights blinking and alarm bells sounding. He liked to close his eyes and pretend. He imagined that Mossy could chase away his pain and he imagined that he was home again.

It made him feel better just to remember being outside in the fresh air, with the warmth of sunshine, the delight of sniffing and smelling the grass, the nearness of birds and butterflies, and the quiet of trees.

The nurses worried that Patch was not healing as he should. The doctors worried that his heart was not strong enough. And Mossy worried most of all.

After tests and talks and more tests, after conferring and consulting among many people, the doctors decided Patch needed a second operation – to give his heart a boost.

Everyone wanted Patch to get better and everyone wanted to help. Doctor Giraffe (with the very l–o–n–g neck) even let Patch listen to his own heartbeat with the stethoscope (a very l–o–n–g word).

A whole team was working together for his benefit. Quiet hopes and songs, and many kindly wishes were offered on his behalf.

This time Patch was not frightened, because he understood what was happening. And this time, in his dreams, a gentle white dog stood by his side and stayed with him, keeping watch until he awoke.

Even after the dream ended, he felt comforted by this special dog.

Just as before, he was at first not well enough to
have visitors. But now his friends also understood
what was happening and were ready with cards
and messages to cheer him. And this time Patch
began to feel better more quickly.

He was soon ready for company again.

First to arrive was the gentle baby panda, quiet and shy. He sat in a corner, spreading calm, as gentle waves spread across the sand.

A parade of other visitors followed – for Patch was known now for being both brave and very patient.

His room became a gathering place – and even
Mother Goose came to visit. She fluffed her feathers
and settled herself down in a motherly way to read
stories.

Like magic, each listener was carried off to a different
world, a world of calm, or fantasy, or adventure. At
these moments, Patch totally forgot that he was in the
hospital.

And then, in no time at all, he was well enough to leave the hospital.

Now he could breathe the fresh air again. He could return with Mossy to their garden with its own special smell of home. They could walk, and soon run, along the beach again – scattering sunlight and seawater. Everything was just as it had been, only better, with more brightness.

Patch's heart filled with happiness. And
Mossy could hardly contain her joy.

Still, they did not forget about their friends
in the hospital. Now it was their turn to send
cards and messages.

Between messages, the puppies made regular
trips to the hospital to visit. Instinctively they
knew who needed them most.

And they knew just what to do to help
someone feel better.

If you are very lucky, perhaps Mossy and Patch will come to visit you.

But even if you do not see them, be sure to know that they are wishing you well and are holding you in their hearts for safekeeping.

Story Notes

This is the story of my own sick puppy, the center of a small circle of concern and affection. Friends, doctors, and nurses do their best to help and, in the end, Patch does recover – in part because of his own sweet and brave nature.

His small patched heart fills with happiness, then overflows with kindness and caring for others. He and his best friend Mossy become therapy dogs.

Their small world is by nature part of a larger community. It is said that one butterfly's wingbeat can affect the air currents of the world. Thus it must be certain that the wagging of one dog's tail in some way touches the life of a community.

———————————

A large circle of friends contributed to the creation of this story. For introducing me to a new world, I thank my small granddaughter Stella, our own dear heart child; for insights and suggestions, my daughter Sarah, and, for his understanding of animals, my son Toby.

Viveka Janssen, Gretchen Van Meter, Jacqueline Baldwin, and Peggy Hutchison offered ideas and encouragement. Dr. Donald Wilson and Dr. Lesley Langford contributed veterinary advice.

Friesens, my printers, provided excellent service and assistance as always. To all of you, thank you.